the Boy who Sailed the World

Julia Green

Alex Latimer

d|b FICKLING

David Fickling Books

Right from the start,
the boy loved the sea!

He ran along the sand,
danced in and out of the waves,
his heart full of longing and delight.

The books he loved best at bedtime
told tales of SEA ADVENTURES.

'I will build me a boat
to sail the seven seas

and have adventures
of my own.'

Away he sailed in his beautiful boat.
He left land far behind.

Evening fell and the boy lost his way but he didn't give up.

'I will set the compass to show me where to go.'

The first star came out and a full moon shone a silver path to guide him on.

Now the sea currents were strong.
The boy was scared.
Big ferries and cargo ships
crossed back and forth.

'I will follow my sea-charts
and bravely steer
through the shipping lanes
safe to the other side.'

On he sailed,
where the sea was blue blue blue
and the sun shone warm.

He watched magical sunsets
and dawn each day
was like the beginning of a new world.

The boy saw no one.
No other boats.
Not even an aeroplane in the sky.

He was all alone.

But a leatherback turtle swam slowly by
and kept him company for a while.

Dolphins dived in the bow wave of the boat.

The boy touched their smooth skin,
heard the click of their song
and sang along.

He learned to listen
to each tiny change to wind and waves,
as if he and the boat were one.

Late one night the boy woke up.

What was that new sound?

A sudden storm
whipped the waves high as hills.
Water swept over the boat.
The wind shrieked.
It ripped the sails, unleashed the ropes.

The boat tipped . . .

There was nothing he could do . . .

'I will trust my boat
through the buffeting storm.'
And the boy clung on.

At last the wind died down
and the sea was calm.

He mended the sail . . .

And the boy sailed on.

For days and weeks
he saw nothing
but ocean.

'I will study the patterns of stars at night
like the old sailors in the stories I love.'

On and on and further still
he sailed,

one ocean to the next,
until

he longed to feel land beneath his feet.

'I will anchor my boat
on a sheltered island
fringed by a shallow reef.'

He made new friends
on their island home.

They fished and swam,
and when the sun went down
they cooked their meal
on a driftwood fire,
and played and sang

and slept the night
under a million trillion stars.

But the echo of a voice he loved
was calling him . . .

The boy waved goodbye,
climbed back on his boat.

'Time to sail back
and tell my tale.

How I dared to dream,
was brave and bold,
trusted myself
when all seemed lost,

left land behind and steered
by the stars
and never gave up . . .

How I looked with wonder
at the world

and made new friends
on far away shores

and then returned . . .

Home

Until my journeys start again . . .'

The world is a BIG place.

So much to see and explore.

What's your dream?

Where will you go?

This story is inspired by a real boy. His name is Jesse and he is my son. When he was a child, he had a dream that one day he would sail around the world. With a friend, he bought an old boat and mended it. They called the boat *Sparrow*. They sailed down the Irish Sea, across the English Channel, the Bay of Biscay, crossed the Atlantic Ocean, then through the Panama Canal and into the Pacific Ocean. They lived for nine months on a tiny remote island called Taravai in the Gambier Archipelago in the French Polynesian islands. Now Jesse is a traditional boat builder. He loves the sea and swims and sails and surfs. He had a dream and he made it come true.

Julia Green